by David Mark Lopez

Hope your life is full of adventure like Maddie's.

DmL

To Maddie, my intrepid traveler, on her 11ᵗʰ birthday

Red Marker Episode

1

Maddie's Magic Markers

Walk Like an Egyptian

Read it Again
3630 Peachtree Pkwy., Ste 314
Suwanee, GA 30024
770-232-9331
www.Read-it-Again.com

D1314689

Maddie's Magic Markers Series
Red Marker (One)
Walk Like An Egyptian
Copyright 2004 by David Mark Lopez
ISBN # 0-9744097-0-7
ISBN # 978-0-9744097-0-2
Library of Congress Control Number: 2003096017

Published by David Mark Lopez
Bonita Springs, FL

All rights reserved. No part of this publication may be reproduced or stored in a retrieval system or transmitted in any form by means of electronic, mechanical, photocopy, recording or by wire without the permission of the publisher except as provided by USA copyright law.

Story and Illustrations by David Mark Lopez
Cover Illustration / Book Design by Jeff Thompson
Printed in the United States of America

What Kids (And Parents) Are Saying About Walk Like an Egyptian!

You made the book exciting to learn about Egypt instead of a learning book that is boring and hard.

- Audra

I can't wait until you make more sequels. Keep writing and making books.

- Shirley

This is a funny and exciting book filled with all kinds of magical and historical characters.

- Shelly

I usually don't like reading, but this book was a very good one and actually got my attention.

- Kayla

I read your book and I loved it! It was one of the best books I have ever read. I couldn't put it down - I just had to find out if she would ever get home!

- Catherine

I wanted to let you know, John plowed through the book you gave me. He was up at 6:00 this morning to finish it before school.

- John's Mom

Ashton started reading your book yesterday and she can't put it down. She absolutely loves it.

- Ashton's Mom

Maddie's Magic Markers

Red Marker (One)

Walk Like An Egyptian

by David Mark Lopez

Table of Contents

Chapter 1
My Boring Life 7

Chapter 2
Never Smile at a Crocodile 13

Chapter 3
Injured, Wet, Hungry & Lost 19

Chapter 4
Hail (Little) Caesar 25

Chapter 5
Confusement 31

Chapter 6
Sit Down! You're Rocking the Boat! 37

Chapter 7
The Queen Bee 43

Chapter 8
A Royal Mess 49

Chapter 9
Oh for Goodness Snakes 55

Table of Contents
(continued)

Chapter 10
Library Card 61

Chapter 11
Sounds Like a Plan 67

Chapter 12
There and Back Again 73

Chapter 1

My Boring Life

My name is Maddisen Tucker, but most people usually just call me Maddie. Sometimes when my dad is trying to be funny (he's not), he calls me Maggie. Most of the time I live in Atlanta with my mom, but every other weekend I go to visit my dad in McIntosh, Florida. My dad is more than just a little weird, but like he says: you only get to pick one family member-the rest of them just show up.

Anyway, until my 10th birthday my life was pretty normal and mostly boring. I mean when the most exciting part of your day is waiting for Jordan, my demented classmate, to pick his nose and eat it that's pretty sad, right? Some of the time when I visit my dad we try to do something "fun" like going to Universal Studios® or go to the movies, but most of the time he just comes into my room and bothers me like this:

"Hey Maggie, what do you want for your big, exciting 10th birthday?"
"I don't know."
"How about a pony?"
"Fine."
"Maybe we could go to Italy and have lunch with the Pope."

"No, thanks."

"I think your Barbies® need some more clothes. I mean ten thousand outfits are not nearly enough. Or maybe a brush and you could brush their hair once."

"Go away."

So anyway when my birthday finally rolled around I got some pretty cool stuff: a new bike, Barbie® stuff, some clothes, a book about Egypt (my dad is always buying me educational stuff), and some antique magic markers, but no pony. So I say:

"Hey dad, where's the pony?"

"Back in your room."

"You're lying."

"Am not."

Of course he was, but I went to check anyway. With my dad you never know. Once I found Santa Claus in the computer room, but that's another story. I took all my birthday stuff back to my room (pony free), read some about Cleopatra and King Tut, and watched a Disney® Movie on T.V. I'd already seen seven other times. It's so good. Since it was my birthday I got to stay up as late as I wanted, so I got around to the magic markers around 11:00.

Everyone knows I like to draw, so I get pens and markers all the time, but I had never seen anything like these in my entire life. First, the case they were in was heavy, solid, reddish wood with thick, brass hinges and a solid brass clasp. The top of the box was engraved with the words "Drawing to the Music of Time". I had no idea what that meant or where my dad found these pens, but he didn't get them at Target®. When you opened the clasp, each marker was encased in heavy, green, embroidered velvet. There were twelve pens in all, and when I removed the first pen it was so heavy I almost dropped it. Cool.

The pen had a thick, silver, metal cap with an engraved clip of intricate design. The middle part of the pen was clear glass and you could see the marker liquid floating inside, flecked with specks of silver and gold and bubbles like Grammie's Christmas bulbs. Each pen was full of dark, rich ink: purple, green, red, orange, yellow, twelve in all. I couldn't wait to draw something.

I sat down at my desk, got out some paper and tried to open the red pen. No luck. No matter how hard I tried, I could not get the cap off. I decided it was time to get my dad involved.

"Hey, Dad."
"I'm sleeping."
"Hey, Dad." I shook him.
"I'm still sleeping."
"Dad, I can't get the cap off."
"What cap?"

"Off the pen."

"What pen?"

"The pens you got me for my birthday."

"Who are you?"

"Dad!!"

"Did you say the magic words?"

"What magic words?"

"The lady at the antique store said you had to say the magic words before you could use the pens."

"OK, so what are the magic words?"

"My dad is awesome."

"Nuh-uh."

"OK, what you really need is a cloak of invisibility."

"Dad, you have slobber on your face."

"Or maybe it was a ring that makes you disappear when you put it on."

"Go back to sleep."

"I remember now. You have to have a pure heart before you can use the pens."

"Stop it."

As I was leaving his room I heard him mumble,

"Try reading the directions, goofus."

I returned to my room to further inspect the box. Of course there were no directions. I thought about bugging my dad again, but he'd probably say something idiotic like "walk through the back of the wardrobe" or "try the magic key in the cupboard."

to have to figure this out on my own.

I studied the pens. Nothing. I returned to the wooden box. No clues on the bottom. No clues inside. The only thing on the outside of the box was the inscription. "Dance". OK, I knew what that meant. (Surely not that belly-buttoned pop-star thing). "Music" I liked it all: pop, country, classical- my dad took me to see the opera once (Carmen) and I even liked that. "Time" Thinking. Thinking. Thinking. I looked at my Mickey Mouse® watch. I held the pen. I hummed the tune of "Toreadoro". It was midnight, the day of my 10th birthday. The cold floor felt good on my bare feet. I closed my eyes and danced to the tune I hummed, clutching the pen and my trusty watch. I stopped dancing when I heard the pen cap clatter on the floor. Easy enough.

When I sat down at my desk I noticed some strange things about the marker. First, the translucent ink floating in the glass part of the pen was glowing like some kind of phosphorescent liquid. Second, I began to notice a subtle aroma emanating from the point of the pen. Nothing unpleasant like the odors frequently emanating from my dad, but like nothing I had ever smelled before. Little did I know that these markers were magical. My boring life was about to be turned upside down.

The red marker left a beautiful, dark stream of red

The red marker left a beautiful, dark stream of red ink on the blank page. I couldn't waste this extraordinary marker on smiley faces, so I began to copy the scene on the cover of my new book. As I began to draw, my head was nodding, my eyelids were closing. The pen grew heavy in my hand and I drifted off to sleep. I swear I saw my dad waving goodbye and saying something I couldn't quite understand.

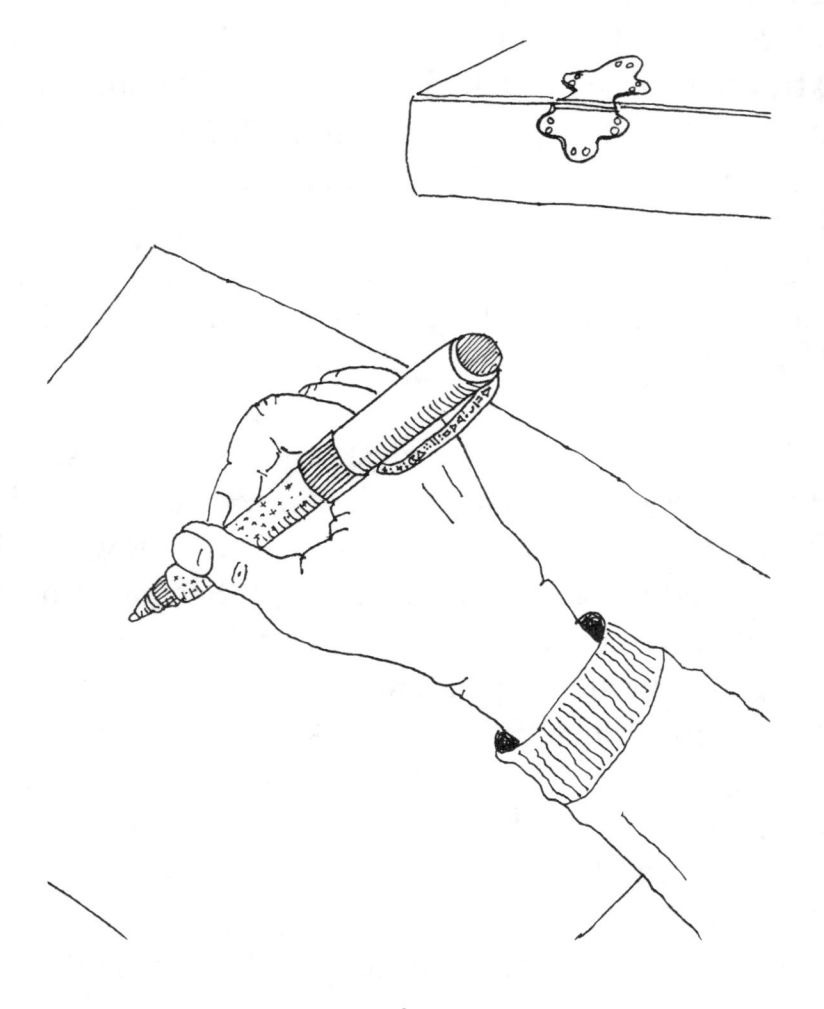

Chapter 2

Never Smile at a Crocodile

When I woke up I immediately noticed several problems. First, I was standing chest deep in slowly moving dark water. Second, I was in my flannel Winnie-the-Pooh pajamas. Finally, and more troubling about eight feet away, half-submerged in water, between me and the shore was something that looked suspiciously like the head of a crocodile. (I know what you're thinking. How did you know it was a crocodile and not an alligator? Hey, I live in Florida - I know what an alligator looks like. This was no alligator.) If his head was any indication, he was a very, very large crocodile. Most unfortunately, the one eye I could see was wide open and appeared to be looking straight at me.

Taking these problems in the order I noticed them: #1- water. The good news: I am an excellent swimmer and even actually like the water. The bad news: I gradually realized I was ankle deep in what I hoped was mud and the only place I actually wanted to swim was blocked by a very large and menacing reptile. #2- My p.j.s – other than being out in what was apparently broad daylight this was OK since there didn't seem to be anyone around. Then it occurred to me that swimming in soaking wet flannel against a current was not going to be easy. #3- The crocodile – Like you,

I've seen that crazy crocodile hunter guy on the Animal Planet more than just a few times. That guy is everywhere. They should change their name from Animal Planet to Crocodile Planet. Anyway, you've probably noticed when he's bugging the heck out of the crocs they are always on land - never in the water. I'm guessing the reason for that is people are a lot better on land and crocs are a lot better in water. Which, as you probably recall, is exactly where I was.

As all this was flashing through my mind and I was trying not to cry, I recalled a brief conversation I had with my Dad once at Busch Gardens about alligators.

"Hey, Dad."
"For the 500th time you cannot have any more cotton candy!"
"Stop yelling. That's not what I'm asking."
"What then?"
"What should I do if I'm being chased by an alligator?"
"Run."
"Thanks a lot."
"From side to side."
"Why?"
"The alligator will think you are crazy and leave you alone."
"Can I please have some more cotton candy?"

Actually my dad was right, but for the wrong reason.

It is a well known fact that alligators have short legs and can't change directions easily. What did I know about crocodiles from my endless hours of watching television? They are very aggressive, have powerful jaws, have that lower 4th tooth thing and have short legs. Bingo. Thank you Steve Irwin. I knew if I could just get to shore I would probably be all right.

Uh oh. Mr. Croc just blinked, so he had to be awake and with my luck was probably hungry. I had to come up with something fast. Points in my favor:

1. The water was warm.
2. It was daylight.
3. I was smarter than the crocodile.

Points in his favor:

1. Natural born predator.
2. Excellent swimmer.
3. Who needs brains with jaws like those?

If the crocodile was hungry I knew I didn't have much time, because it was more than clear that he had seen me. I had to do something fast or my short but happy life was over. Slowly I pulled one foot and then another out of the muck surrounding my feet. Did he just blink again? I lowered my head down to eye level with the croc and began to let myself float in the current. I glanced backward toward the croc just in time to see his massive tail flick like a gigantic serpent. I could have peed my pants if I wasn't so scared. Still I did not panic. I closed my eyes, held my breath and swam down with the current towards the bank (I was only guessing). My heart was pounding so hard I could feel it up in my ears. I wanted to open my eyes, but I just couldn't make myself do it. I held my breath and swam below the surface until my lungs felt like they were going to explode. I could feel the bottom of the river with my hands so I knew I had to be close to shore. I stood up on my knees as I broke the surface gasping for air and instantly looked back to where the crocodile had been floating. Bad, really bad news. He was gone.

I struggled to my feet and lunged toward the shore. When I was about three feet from freedom the croc burst out of the water with an awesome, furious snap just missing my right arm, but cutting me off from the shore line. No time to think, just move. While he gathered himself for another attack I ran and jumped and crawled back in the direction where I came from. As he turned to his left I tried to jump over his massive tail and he whipped me into the shallow water. I splashed and crawled left then right, left then right quickly changing directions, but I knew he was closing fast. As I leaped on to the shore I heard his jaw snap again and I felt a sharp, stabbing pain in my left calf. Horrified, I turned to see he had my pajama leg in his mouth. I dove toward higher ground and instinctively grabbed the first thing I could find - a stick about the size of a baseball bat. Crawling backwards, I pounded the croc's massive snout repeatedly with the log and screamed every bad word I knew at him. Finally when he opened his mouth (to get a better grip no doubt), I jammed the stick into his mouth and scrambled further away from the water. He must have figured out that I was more trouble than I was worth, because he only followed me a few steps before retreating back to the dark water. Before I left that beast for good I noticed the stick was broken into pieces. The monster probably wasn't used to having his dinner whack him on the head. Walnut Brain.

When I felt safe I sat down on a rock. As the adrenaline pumping in my veins receded and my normal breathing pattern returned I began to cry. I'm no baby and I almost never cry (except once when my dad flicked me really hard with a wet towel), but things were looking really bad. My left calf was bleeding steadily from the croc bite. I was shivering in my soaking wet pajamas. Then the scariest thing of all slowly crept into my mind. I had no earthly idea of what time it was, what day it was or where I was.

Chapter 3
Injured, Wet, Hungry & Lost

It didn't take me long to figure out that crying wasn't going to get me anywhere, so I wiped the snot off my face with the back of my hand and took a long look at my left calf. It hurt and was bleeding pretty good, but it wasn't too deep, and I figured I was going to live. I tore off the rest of my p.j. leg, wrung out the water and tied it around the wound. I knew I would need to clean it better, but that was going to have to do for now.

Now to the larger problems. I was starting to get hungry, I was still in my wet p.j.s and where in the world was I? Below me I could see the wide river, broad and flat stretching in both directions as far as I could see. Behind me were some good sized hills. Judging by the position of the sun it was still morning, warm enough, but starting to get hot, so I knew I would dry out soon. There was no sign of civilization and there was no sign of anything that looked remotely like food.

What I needed now was a plan. No way was I going back to the river with Señor Croc and who knows what else waiting for me. I decided my best bet was to follow the river (at a safe distance) until I found something or someone. I looked at the river again and decided to go in the same direction as the current. It occurred to me with the position of the sun in my eyes that the river was flowing north. Don't most rivers flow south? That's something my Dad would know. He is full of useless information.

"Hey Maddie."
"Dad, I'm trying to read."
"Did you know that we live in Florida?"
"Duh."
"Did you know that the St. John's River in Florida
  flows north?"
"and…"
"Most rivers in the Northern Hemisphere flow
  south."
"Fascinating."

This could only mean one thing: either I was in the southern half of the world or there were crocodiles in the St. John's River.

Well none of this was getting me any closer to much needed food and medical attention, so I decided to get moving. I hobbled further up the bank, noticed something that looked vaguely like a path and set off; leg throbbing, belly empty, p.j.s slowly drying, barefoot and limping.

I followed the path that ran along the river, slowly drying out and gradually coming to my senses. I tried to remember everything that happened before I fell asleep: my birthday party, the presents, my dad, the pens. I thought about the pens so hard that my head started hurting, but I just couldn't figure it out. One possible explanation was that I was dreaming, but people don't bleed in their dreams, do they? I knew I wasn't dreaming because everything was so terribly real.

After about an hour walking, I stopped to rest and check out my leg. I unwrapped the wet, bloody bandage for a closer look. The bleeding had pretty much stopped, but I knew it had to be cleaned. I reluctantly tiptoed back to the river and cleaned out the wound and the wet bandage, keeping one eye on the river at all times. Wow - a couple of more inches and I'd be missing half a leg. I went back up the bank, sat down and tore off the other leg of my now dry pajamas. I wrapped my calf with the dry material and laid the wet bandage out to dry.

Do you ever get a funny feeling that someone is watching you? In the entire time I was walking I hadn't seen anything but a few birds and some scrawny lizards, but I knew at that very moment I was being watched.

I looked back up and down the river carefully and to my surprise about half way across in the water directly in front of me I noticed three sets of large pinkish eyes and three sets of purplish ears. I was somewhat relieved that these were not crocodiles, but I must have jumped a half a foot when one set of these eyes and ears rose out of the water blowing and bellowing. After I landed and realized I wasn't in any real danger, it came to me that I was looking at a herd of hippos. It was now official then that I was not dreaming - no one dreams about hippos except other hippos and zoo keepers.

I watched the hippos for awhile at a safe distance, but since I had already had enough animal adventures for one day I decided to move on. As I left the hippos behind I reached a stunning conclusion – the only place you could find hippos were at the zoo and in Africa. This clearly wasn't a zoo. I had woken up in Africa and I was now traveling north on the west bank of what had to be the Nile River and I was a very long, long way from home.

Now that I got all that straight I had to find some food. I knew it was lunch time, because I almost never eat breakfast and I start getting ravenous around noon. Here's how it usually goes:

"Good morning, Maddie."
"Mmmmm…"
"What would you like for breakfast?"
"Nothing."
"You need to eat something."
"What do we have?"
"How about some cereal?"
"What kind?"
"Lucky Charms, Cocoa Puffs, Cheerios, Chex,

Frosted Flakes, Raisin Bran, Golden Crisp, Honey Comb or dried booger flakes."

"I'm not hungry."

"You at least have to drink some milk."

"Why?"

"Osteoporosis."

"Chocolate?"

"No."

"What's osteoporosis?"

"Brittle bones."

"I don't have brittle bones."

"And I don't want you to have them, so that's why you need to drink the milk."

"Oh."

"Now what do you want to eat?"

"What else do we have?"

"It doesn't matter."

"Why not?"

"Because I'm going to kill you long before you have to worry about osteoporosis."

So anyway Dad gets distracted and forgets about my breakfast and doesn't remember I have not eaten anything until about noon, so then I just have lunch (with milk). That's why I never eat breakfast, but right now I probably could have eaten those dried booger flakes I was so hungry. I did, however momentarily stop thinking about food when I heard someone say,

"Bow down and worship me."

Chapter 4
Hail (Little) Caesar

It was starting to get really hot out and like I mentioned a few times earlier I hadn't had anything to eat or drink all day, so I wasn't exactly sure if I had heard what I thought I heard until I heard it again.

"Bow down and worship me."

Louder this time. Now that's not a phrase you hear everyday unless you live with my dad (he's always trying to get me to do something stupid for ice cream). I hurried to the next ridge where I thought the voice came from and crawled on my belly to where I could see but not be seen. No reason to take any chances if I really was in Africa.

What I saw was more than just a little surprising. About fifty yards away in a gully below me were two children: a completely naked little boy with a strange haircut holding a wooden sword and thrusting it at a strangely dressed girl wearing sandals. She looked to be about my age or maybe a little older. He thrust the sword and shouted,

"I said bow down and worship me!"
"And I said if you poke me again you little barbarian,

I'll rip off your sidelock and strangle you with it."

He thrust and she jumped out of the way and tried to grab his arm. He spun loose and whacked her on the butt as he ran away.

"Die, evil Queen of the Nile."
"Come back here, you jackal."

The boy dodged and darted, thrusting his sword and just managing to avoid the girl's grasp. She finally stopped chasing him and bent over to grab her knees and rest. She was gasping for air.

"We have to get back to camp. If you do not come with me I will leave you to die in the desert. The lions and wolves will fight over your puny body."

The small boy dropped his sword dramatically and fell backward into the sand and lay completely still.

"Please don't eat me. Please don't eat me. Please don't eat me."

The girl slowly inched toward him. As she grew closer he began to scoot backwards away from her. She lunged at him and grabbed his ankle, but as she fell forward he twisted away again squealing with delight. Then he started running up the hill straight toward me.

"Not toward the river! Watch out for the crocodiles!"

This time she was not kidding and there was genuine fear in her voice. I knew first hand; or rather first leg what a croc could do. He was still coming right toward me and she was not catching up fast enough. I had to make a decision quickly. I could blow my cover and help her with demon boy, or I could hide and let him run into the river and fend for himself.

As he flew by me, I casually stuck out my good leg and tripped the little hellion. He tumbled head over heels for a few feet and looked genuinely surprised to see me when he finally rolled to a stop. He looked even more surprised when I pounced on him and pinned his skinny arms to the ground. He didn't even struggle. Must have been my blonde hair and the Winnie-the-Pooh p.j.s.

Seconds later the girl topped the hill with her eyes open wide. As she took in what she saw she stopped dead in her tracks and looked at me in relief, amazement and fear.

"Please, please do not hurt him."
"I'm not hurting him, but if I let him go he's just going to run away again."
"If you let him go, my mistress will give you many pieces of gold."

"I don't want any gold, but if you had any control over this brat I wouldn't have to sit on him like this."

Suddenly monkey boy stopped being shy and lurched back to life. He wasn't very big but he was strong, and I knew I couldn't hold him for long. When he kicked my wounded leg I thought I was going to pass out.

"Help me please!"

She must have finally figured out that I wasn't trying to hurt him and that I was trying to help her, so she arrived just as he was getting loose again. We each grabbed a wrist and wrestled him back to the ground. She hissed at him,

"This is your last warning. If you do not calm down I will never, ever take you anywhere outside the camp."

This warning seemed to finally sink into the naked kid because he actually stopped struggling and his arms and legs went limp. Everyone was quiet for a few seconds while we gathered our breath.

I noticed they were both staring at me. The girl had short hair black as night, tanned dark skin and eyes as dark and shiny as marbles. She was obviously glaring at me.

"You do not know what you have done."

"I was only trying to help."

"If you had hurt him, you would be killed."

"And if I would not have stopped him he'd be a crocodile snack right now."

"What is a snack?"

"Comes between breakfast and lunch or lunch and dinner."

"What?"

"Food!"

This seemed to calm her down a little. She thought for a minute. The boy remained calm.

"What are you called?"

"My name is Maddie."

"Mad – die."

"Right, but you say the syllables together, Maddie."

"Maddie."

"Now you are getting it, girl. Who are you?"

"I am called Aida."

"Eye-ee-dah?"

"Yes."

This seemed to break the tension a little and she noticed my now bleeding again left calf. She pointed to my leg.

"You are hurt."

"Yes. I barely got away from an angry crocodile about a mile up the river." I glanced in the direction I had come from.

"Follow me."

"Where are we going?" They were up and moving.

"We must get back to camp and return this evil child to his mother."

"Who is he?"

"Caesarion, son of Julius Caesar."

I was stunned. "And who is his mother?"

She smiled. "Cleopatra, Pharaoh of Egypt."

As Aida and Caesarion disappeared over the ridge, I hobbled after them. I was still hungry and hurting, but now I had bigger troubles. A lot bigger.

Chapter 5
Confusement

As I followed along my head was spinning. Not only had I traveled half way around the world, I had somehow also managed to travel backwards in time. This was so confusing. Julius Caesar and Cleopatra in ancient Egypt? I tried to calculate exactly how far back I had come, but I just couldn't remember from my history class or my museum trips where in time I had landed. The only thing I knew for certain was that it was probably before the time of Christ. Somehow those pens had transported me across an ocean and backwards over 2000 years. I needed a plan to try and get back home, but I couldn't worry about that now. What I needed now was food, water and some medical treatment. My best hope for that was the two Egyptians a few feet in front of me.

"It is not much further now. When we get to camp you must do as I say."

We had continued north along the river in the same direction I had been traveling. It was really starting to warm up and I was getting extremely thirsty. My throat was parched and my mouth was dry.

I reluctantly decided to ask Aida some questions. As

I got closer to her I noticed, along with her simple white outfit, she was wearing a beautiful necklace. Her dress was off-white and looked almost like a t-shirt coming down to her thigh, but the lower half was pleated like a skirt. Around her waist was a belt made of the same pleated material.

"Hey that's a really nice necklace. Where did you get it?"

"It was a present from the Pharaoh."

"What is it made of?"

"Gold, of course."

"And what is that bird hanging on the necklace?"

"It is no bird, you foolish child. It is Re – the falcon headed Sun-God."

"Sorry I asked." This was obviously not going well.

"Why are you camping out?"

"What?"

"You know, living in tents, cooking over fires, toasting marshmallows."

"I do not know what you are speaking of. We have only stopped to camp so the men could hunt in the desert and to replenish our supplies. We get back on the boats tomorrow."

"Where are you going?"

"To Thebes, the Valley of the Kings."

"Where are we now?"

"We have passed the Pyramids, the ancient Sphinx and the great City of Memphis. You should know all these things."

"Why are you going to the valley of the Kings?"

"The Pharaoh seeks wisdom from the ancestors and the Gods of Egypt. Cleopatra knows that Egypt is in grave danger."

"What danger?"

"You ask too many questions. Be silent."

I'm pretty sure she had just told me to shut up, but I decided to keep going.

"Aida, I need your help."

"You will receive food, water and treatment from the royal doctor when we get to camp. The Gods have smiled on you."

Funny, I didn't feel quite so lucky at that moment.

"Aida, that's not what I meant. I need to get back home."

"Where is home?"

"That's really hard to explain and I know you won't believe me, so let's just say I have come from a long, long way."

"Are you a Roman?"

"I don't think so."

"Then what are you?"

I knew it wasn't going to do any good to tell I was an American, or that I was from Georgia or Florida or anyplace she had never heard of.

"I'll have to explain that later. So can you help
me get back home?"
"That is impossible."
"Why?"
"If you cannot tell me where you are from, how
can I help you get back home?"

I noticed Junior (little Caesar) was picking up the
pace, so I guessed we were getting closer to camp.

"Aida, I will tell you the truth. I am going to need
some powerful magic to find my way back home."
"I have no magic."

I must have looked like I was about to cry so she
spoke again.

"Perhaps my mistress, the great Queen of the Nile,
Cleopatra, Pharaoh of Egypt, can help you. You
must seek an audience with her."
"Can you do that for me?"
"Sssshhh."

She put her finger to her lips.

Just at that moment we topped a long ridge we had
been climbing. What I saw below took my breath away.
These Egyptians knew how to camp in style. I saw

dozens and dozens of tents stretching from the river to the desert. There were hundreds of people busily working at various tasks. Some were fishing, some were cooking, some were seeing to the huge long boats docked at the bank, some tended animals and some were pointing and looking right at us.

Junior let out a yelp and headed down the embankment towards the camp. He was greeted warmly by several of the men wearing armor and carrying long spears. Aida and I followed along more slowly, making our way down the steep slope. As we came down a crowd gathered around Caesarion and a lot of them were jabbering excitedly. As we got closer I decided to play it cool and let Aida do the talking. Big mistake.

"Aida, where have you been? Cleopatra is greatly distraught!"
"I'm sorry. I took a walk with Caesarion and he ran away. He kept running and running down the river. I had to follow him, and no one heard me cry for help."

Aida was evidently in some pretty big trouble, and I felt a little sorry for her. If it was her job to keep an eye on Junior she had her hands full. Suddenly I noticed everyone was looking at me.

"And who is this?"
"Seize her."

Next thing you know two of those big guys with the spears are holding me way too tightly by the arms.

"Hey, what's the deal? Let me go. Let me go, I said! Aida, tell them what happened!"
"She attacked Caesarion and I freed him. I have brought her back to camp to be judged."

The whole bad day just came crashing in on me. Lost, injured, hungry, thirsty, confused, and tired. I was going to say something, then things got a little fuzzy and faded to black.

Chapter 6
Sit Down! You're Rocking the Boat!

It was dark when I finally woke up. It felt so wonderful to be back in my bed in McIntosh. My comfortable sheets and warm blanket felt like old friends. It was almost enough to make me forget that weird nightmare I had about Egypt: markers, crocodiles, hippos, Egyptian children, betrayal. When I thought about Aida's betrayal I sat up in bed with a start. It was then I realized to my dismay that I had not been dreaming. This was not my bed. This was not my bedroom. This was not Florida. Darn.

"Lay down, my child. Get some rest."
"Where am I?"
"You are in the safekeeping of Cleopatra VII,
   Pharaoh of Egypt."
"Am I a prisoner?"
"Your fate will be decided tomorrow. You must
   rest for now."
"I am so thirsty."
"There is both water and food beside your bed."

I gulped the water thirstily from the jug near the bed. I drank every single drop and even spilled some of it on myself I was drinking so fast. Whoever was in the room with me quietly filled the jug again. As I drank more slowly this time my thirst began to be quenched.

As my eyes adjusted to the darkness I noticed the tray near my bed also held grapes, bananas and what I hoped was bread. I was starving. I ate the fruit first and it surprised me that it tasted exactly the same as the fruit we get at the grocery store. Amazing. I tried the flat round bread next. I can't say it was the best thing I've ever eaten, but it tasted pretty good just then.

As I lay back in my bed I noticed that my injured leg had been bandaged and didn't seem to hurt like it had before. A little bit of good news for a change.

"Thank you for the food and water. What is your name?"
"They call me Iras."
"Iras, can you tell me what is going to happen to me?"
"Tomorrow, after we leave on the boats you will be judged by the high priest. You must get back to sleep to regain your strength."

I thought about this for a few minutes. What I really needed was a lawyer. Thanks a lot Dad. You are doing me absolutely no good 10,000 miles and 2,000 years away. I was going to have to defend myself. I couldn't wait to cross examine Aida.

"Iras, can I ask you something?"
"If you must."
"Why is Caesarion so important?"

"He is the future of Egypt. He is the future of Rome. It is Cleopatra's great desire when it is time for him to unite and rule the two great empires."

"Where is his father, Julius Caesar?"

Iras was silent. I could tell even in the darkness she was deciding how much information to share with me. Several minutes passed by.

"His father was murdered in Rome on the floor of the Senate. Caesarion and Cleopatra had to flee for their lives. The enemies of Caesar also desire the death of Caesarion."

I thought about these things for a few minutes. It wasn't enough that I had traveled through time. I had landed smack in the middle of a gigantic mess. Cleopatra had more on her mind than helping me with my troubles. I seriously doubted I would get the chance to meet with her. I needed a new plan.

"Iras, when we get on the boats in the morning where are we going?"

"To Thebes, the Valley of the Kings. To the great Temples of Karnak and Luxor."

"How long will it take us?"

"No more questions. Rest now. Your fate will be decided tomorrow."

That was the second time she had said that. I didn't like the sound of it, but I was really sleepy and it wasn't long before I was out cold.

The next morning everything happened in a hurry. Iras woke me and directed me to wash from a large bowl of water near the bed. I also had more fruit including some figs (not bad). There was also some mystery meat, but when she told me it was heron I decided to pass. She gave me a dress like the one Aida wore yesterday: a simple lightweight cotton thingy. No sign of my Winnie-the-Pooh p.j.s, but I still had my underwear, thank goodness for that, because the dress was a little big and a bit breezy.

When we emerged from the tent it was daylight. The camp was completely transformed from what I had seen the day before. Everything had been taken down and was being loaded onto the boats. I must have slept soundly, because I had not heard any of this early morning activity. There was so much confusion and activity I thought about making a run for it, but I decided I had a better chance with humans than with wild animals.

The boat I was led to was long and narrow with large, long oars on each side. The oars were up though and sails were being hoisted as we boarded. Part of the boat was covered and part of the boat was in the open. I sat silently in the open part of the boat while the men finished loading. No sign of Aida, Junior or anyone who could have been Cleopatra. I was definitely not riding on the first class boat. We set sail.

I didn't have much time to enjoy the scenic river cruise. Just a few minutes after we shoved off the door to the closed part of the boat opened and a tall man in a purple robe came striding out. He had on a lot of jewelry, a really funky hat, some seriously curly, long, dark hair and a very stern look. Had to be the priest. My "trial" was about to begin. As he stood in front of me several of the men and women gathered around. Everyone was looking at you-know-who.

"You are Mad-die?"
"Actually it's Maddie, all one word. And who are you?"
"Silence! You only answer my questions; you do not ask me questions."

So much for due process of law.

"You are charged with attempting to harm the son of the Pharaoh. I have spoken with Aida and have found you to be guilty. The only thing remaining to decide is whether you will live or die."

This was not going well at all and obviously I was not going to get the chance to explain what really happened. It was time for something really dramatic.

"So Maddie, you of golden hair and bright, blue eyes, you are certainly not an Egyptian. Before I decide your fate you must tell me from where you have come."

I gulped and swallowed hard summoning up my courage and my loudest voice.

"I am Maddisen, Goddess of the Hippopotamus (sounded good) sent from the Heavens to warn Cleopatra of her fate with the Romans!"

You could have heard a pin drop.

Chapter 7
The Queen Bee

I later found out that the Egyptians have Gods for just about everything: cats, wolves, falcons, dogs, crocodiles, lions, the sun, floods, all the forces of nature, Gods of Upper Egypt, Gods of Lower Egypt. Hey they probably had a God for nose hair for all I knew. The point is, with over seven hundred Gods in all they probably already had a God of the hippos and he/she in all likelihood didn't look anything like me.

The way old curly locks the priest was looking at me I knew that he was more than just a little suspicious, but I had everyone's attention so I just kept rolling.

"The Gods have sent me to warn you of the great and terrible things that await the Egyptians. They have sent me to deliver a message of great importance to Cleopatra and her people. They have sent me to bring news of the Romans."

I think it was the part about the Romans that put me over the top. When I said that, everyone started murmuring and tall man looked a little flustered. I didn't really care about the Hippo Goddess part as long as I got to see Cleopatra and give her my side of the story.

"Follow me."

I followed the Priest through the door, giving a little wave to my fans as I passed by. They had obviously never seen a Goddess quite like me.

The Priest sat me down quite hard on a chair. He was obviously perturbed.

"All right Goddess of the Hippopotamus, tell me what you know about the Romans."
"I can only give the message to Cleopatra."
"Tell me and your life will be spared."
"If you kill me Cleopatra will never get the message."
"If you give me the message I will give it to Cleopatra."
"If I give you the message I will have to kill you."
"If you kill me how will I give the message to Cleopatra?"
"Exactly."

After this exchange we were both really confused, but he was apparently giving up. He took me back outside and I watched Egypt float by as we sailed up the Nile. I had lots of time to sit and think.

Later that afternoon I was transported to another boat which it didn't take me long to figure out was Cleopatra's. Now I was riding in first class. After some lunch - more fruits and vegetables but once again I declined the mystery meat - I was escorted by the priest to the interior of the boat. I tried to figure out what exactly I was going to say, but I couldn't come up with anything brilliant.

The room was basically filled with people, guards, more priests, servants and oh yeah, the Queen of Egypt. When I entered the room she was laughing pleasantly, so that made me feel a little more at ease. She was lounging in something that looked like a cross between a couch and a bed. When I finally got a good look at her I couldn't take my eyes off of her. She wasn't what I would call beautiful, but she was captivating. Her long, white robe was sheer and elegant. Her jewelry was gold and stunning – broad bands decorated with precious stones around her neck and arms. She wore a simple tiara with an amulet of a sphinx in the center. Her makeup was beautiful and she carried herself with great confidence and composure. She looked and acted like a Queen.

"So this is our latest Goddess of Egypt. Come and sit beside me Goddess Maddie for my priest tells me you bring important news."
"Actually, I wanted to tell you about Caesarion and Aida first. It was all a terrible mistake. I wasn't trying to hurt your son; I was trying to keep him from being eaten by the crocodiles."

I must have started babbling incoherently at this point, because she gently patted my hand and looked into my eyes and smiled.

"Try to calm down my child. I know you have been falsely accused. Aida broke down and told me the whole story last night. She could not bear to see you punished for something you did not do. I know how difficult Caesarion can be and you have done me a great service. You are to be honored."

"There's something else I need to tell you. I'm not really a goddess and I don't actually know anything about the Romans. I just made all that up so I could get the chance to speak with you."

"I once made a dramatic entry myself for the chance to meet Julius Caesar. My enemies did not want me to meet him, so I had myself wrapped in a carpet and delivered to him. He was very surprised when I came tumbling out of a rug."

She smiled to herself and looked off at some point in the distance. When she sighed I knew it might be a good time to change the subject, since the last news I heard about Julius Caesar was not good at all.

"Your Majesty, I needed to talk to you for another reason. I have a very difficult problem that I need your help with."

"Yes, what is it?"

"I don't know how I got here to Egypt. I fell asleep and I woke up in the river. I have come from such a long way, and I don't know how to get back home. Can you please help me?"

"You do not like it here in Egypt in the company of the Pharaoh?"

"Yes, it all seems very nice and I would love to stay, but I have to get back to my family and to school. I cannot stay in Egypt because I do not belong here."

"How can I help you then?"

"I need some magic to get me back. You are the ruler of Egypt - the most powerful woman in the world. You must be able to tell me something."

"This is a most serious problem and one that I do not have the answer to. Alas, Egypt is also in a difficult situation. If I think about how to solve your problem, perhaps you could agree to think about mine."

"What is it?"

"Egypt has been a great civilization for over three thousand years. We have long been one of the richest and most powerful peoples in the entire world. But now because of the strength of the Romans we are to become Roman subjects. My husband Julius Caesar has been murdered. I once dreamed of a mighty empire; a united Rome and Egypt ruled by my son, Caesarion, but now those dreams are dead. I have been summoned to meet with a new Roman leader Mark Antony and he is to decide the fate of my people, the fate of Egypt. We go to Thebes, the Valley of the Kings to seek the wisdom of the ancestors."

"So how can I help?"

"Maddie, you say you come from a far off place. From where you come from, what would be the best way to seek the blessing and good graces of Mark Antony? If you will help me with my problem I will help you with yours. Fair enough?"

"Yes, Pharaoh."

"In the meantime Maddie, Goddess of the Hippopotamus, you must be punished for deceiving my people."

Uh-oh. This might not be so good.

"You must help Aida watch Caesarion and see that no harm befalls him."

"Wait a minute."

"Besides, I knew you could not be a true goddess."

"Why not?"

"Goddesses do not get half eaten by crocodiles!"

She had me on that one.

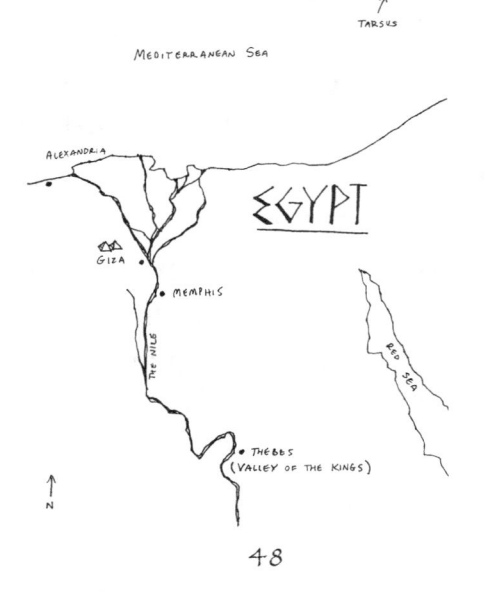

Chapter 8
A Royal Mess

I can't say I really liked my new assignment, but it was way better than being a prisoner or worse. After we got to know each other Aida and I became friends. She confessed that the only reason she lied about me was to keep everyone from realizing it was she who had let Junior wander off. We were both under the supervision of Iras: one of Cleopatra's most important servants and the one who had helped me that first night.

We reached the Valley of the Kings in a couple of days. In talking with Aida I learned much about the Egyptian way of life. Everyone was very worried about Cleopatra's decision. I also learned that after Julius Caesar's death the Roman Empire was divided among its three leaders: Lepidus, Octavian and Antony. Antony had chosen Egypt because of her wealth and had sent for Cleopatra to meet him at a city called Tarsus.

When we left the boat and made camp at Thebes I was stunned. The temples at Luxor and Karnak were awesome. Luxor was built by Ramses, the greatest of all Egyptian Pharaohs. The temple at Karnak was home to Amnon, the ruler God of Upper Egypt. It was the largest building I have ever been in. All the walls, tall structures and huge monuments were covered with

Egyptian writing. Connecting the two temples were rows of ram-headed sphinxes. It was amazing.

I wish I would have had more time to look around and ask questions, but Aida and I spent most of our time chasing Caesarion. Since he was the son of the Pharaoh, he could do no wrong, and it was our job to keep him out of trouble. That wasn't too hard to accomplish when we were sailing up the river, but once we got on land it was a whole 'nother story. This kid never took a nap and spent most of his waking hours trying to ditch us.

We spent three days at Thebes, and during the late afternoon of the third day Aida came running breathlessly into our tent. Most of the time we both watched Little Caesar, but every once in a while we took turns giving each other a break. From the look on Aida's face I could tell something was terribly wrong.

"Maddie, come quickly! I've lost him!"
"What do you mean?"
"I can't find him. We were playing by the rocks and he just disappeared."
"How long has he been gone?"
"Only a short while, but it will be dark soon. Quickly, we must find him!"

That was the understatement of the century (whichever one we were in). There was no way either of us could afford to be in trouble with Cleopatra again. Besides, she had enough to worry about without a missing heir to the throne. We had to find Caesarion and bring him back before anyone found out.

I quickly followed Aida out of the tent. We grabbed a couple of torches as we left camp. Darkness was falling as we headed out into the desert.

We had been warned many times about wandering away from camp at night because of the jackals. I definitely was not too thrilled about being out alone in the desert at night, but I tried not to think about it. I followed Aida for about ten minutes until we reached the place she had last seen Caesarion.

Rocks, rocks and more rocks. We called for him over and over, but there was no response. I was beginning to think the worst had happened until I noticed a small opening to the side of the hill where several odd shaped stones came together. I motioned for Aida to come and take a look. The opening was just large enough for a small boy to fit through.

As luck would have it the opening was also just large enough for me to fit into, but not Aida. I stuck both the torch and my head in partway. I called for Caesarion and I thought I heard something like a child crying but I wasn't sure because of the echoes. I didn't really want to crawl into that dark place, but it was that or go back and tell Cleopatra we'd lost her son.

When I got through the opening and my eyes adjusted to the flickering light on the walls thrown by my torch, I noticed I was standing at the top of a staircase. I carefully followed the steps down, about ten or twelve in all to a passageway. The sound of the crying though muffled was louder. I walked slowly and cautiously down the passageway to where it ended. There were several loose stones the size of small blocks covering an entrance to another room. A couple of them had been removed. I stuck my torch through the opening. I couldn't believe my eyes.

The room was completely filled with stuff. Really old stuff. Most of it was covered in gold and it was piled high to the ceiling: chariots, wheels, beds, statues, a throne, weapons, dishes, pots, you name it.

I stepped gently and cautiously into the room. I discovered treasures beyond my wildest imagination. As my eyes adjusted to the light it became apparent I had stumbled into a royal tomb. Then I heard the crying even louder.

"Caesarion, is that you?"
"Aida?"
"No, it's Maddie. Where are you?"
"Back here."

I noticed that at the far end of the room was another doorway. On each side of the door were two large ebony statues. I slowly stepped between them into the next room. The room was almost completely filled with something I immediately recognized from the book my dad gave me: the burial sarcophagus of the boy King of Egypt, Tutankhamen. I was in the tomb of King Tut. Unbelievable.

As all of this dawned on me, out of the corner of my eye I saw Caesarion crouched in the corner, his face streaked with tears. Just as I was about to speak to him, I noticed the fanned head of the cobra a few feet from him. The torch flickered once and then went out. Oh boy.

Chapter 9
Oh for Goodness Snakes

Three things:

1. It was really dark. Not the kind of dark when your dad shuts out the light when it's time for bed and you can still make out a few things. It was pitch black. My dad took me to the Florida Caverns near Tallahassee once and when we got down into the caves the guide turned off all the lights. You couldn't even see your hand in front of your face. That's how dark it was.

2. How did that cobra get down into the tomb? My first thought was that it had been left there to guard the treasure. That probably wasn't true though, because it couldn't have survived all those years without any food or water. Most likely it had made its way down into the tomb the same way Caesarion had - bad luck and being too nosy for its own good.

3. Snakes in general. I'm not some kind of screaming baby when it comes to snakes, but I have a healthy respect for them. I knew cobras were highly poisonous, but I also remember what my dad had taught me about snakes. They are more scared of you than you are of them, and if you leave them alone they'll probably leave you alone. I just hoped that

my cobra pal hadn't brought his family along for a picnic.

I slowly bent down and scooped up some sand in my hand. Caesarion began whimpering again, but he stopped when I shushed him. I moved ever so slowly in the direction where I thought he was sitting. With one swift motion I threw the sand toward the cobra, hoped some got in his eyes and grabbed Caesarion. When the cobra slithered across my feet I completely lost it. I pulled Caesarion along with me into the treasure room. He was crying and I was screaming. We both fell down a couple of times and probably knocked over half the stuff in the room.

I somehow made it back to the passageway, and I could hear Aida calling at the top of the stairs. I heard some stones falling behind us and I scrambled up the stairs dragging the boy wonder behind me. When I got to the top of the stairs I pushed Caesarion through the hole and I wasted no time following him. I couldn't wait to get out of there.

"Oh, Maddie. What has happened?"

I decided to keep my discovery a secret, so I didn't say a word. I found some rocks big enough to block the opening and carefully closed the hole. King Tut would be safe for another 2,000 years I hoped.

I muttered something about snakes and we made our way back to camp. Caesarion was tired and upset, so we took turns carrying him and the fast fading torch. We somehow managed to get him back to our tent without anyone realizing we were gone. My heart finally stopped pounding when we lay down to sleep. A sandstorm blew all night and I dreamed of Tutankhamen.

When we got up the next morning I knew his burial chambers would be safe for decades to come. Six inches of sand had covered everything in the camp. As I got dressed Aida noticed that something was stuck in the material on the back of the cotton dress I wore the night before.

"What is it?"

We both stared in wonder. Attached to the back of my dress was a beautiful piece of Egyptian jewelry. It was a solid gold scarab with wings outstretched for several inches. The wings were inlaid glass stones of red, blue, turquoise and green. When I delicately removed it from the dress I discovered it was a bracelet. The wings of the scarab folded around my wrist. Aida was impressed.

"The Gods have smiled on you Maddie. Perhaps you will make it home after all."

If she suspected what I had found in the tomb she hid it well. In fact she never mentioned what happened that night ever again. One thing was certain though: part of the treasure of Tutankhamen was on my wrist and it was never going back. Maybe it would bring me good luck.

We broke camp and returned to the boats. It would take two weeks to float back down the Nile to Alexandria. We also floated past the place where I met Aida and Little Caesar. We floated past the place I had encountered the crocodile (no sign of that joker). I looked carefully for any clues that might tell me how I ended up there and more importantly how I might get home, but there was nothing. I began to wonder if I would ever make it home again.

The days passed by quickly and pleasantly. I learned many things about the history and culture of Egypt from Aida and Iras. Cleopatra was greatly loved and respected by her people, because of her deep devotion and passion for her land. There was no indication of whether or not she had made a decision about Mark Antony. I thought long and hard about her problem. I hoped she was thinking long and hard about mine.

After a few days we floated by the Great Pyramids of Egypt and the Sphinx. I was told they were over 2,000 years old and were tombs for the first Pharaohs. The later Pharaohs were buried in the Valley of the Kings because grave robbers had plundered the tombs of the pyramids. They thought if they were buried in a more remote place their treasures would be safe. The reason all those things were placed in the tombs was to assist the Pharaoh in the afterlife. That plan didn't work either. All of the tombs in the Valley of the Kings had been plundered as far as anyone knew. All but one, anyway.

As we got closer and closer to Alexandria I wondered more and more about my future. Was I destined to spend the rest of my life as an Egyptian in Cleopatra's court? Was I ever going to see my friends and family again? Would my dad give away all my toys?

I still didn't have any answers when the priest motioned for me to follow him.

"Cleopatra has requested your presence."

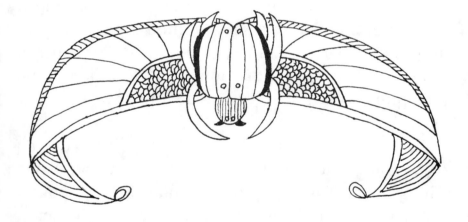

Chapter 10
Library Card

This time my meeting with Cleopatra was much more private. There were only a couple of servants in the room when I was taken into her chambers. She was dressed informally with almost no jewelry and very little make up. I was much more relaxed this time and was actually looking forward to speaking with her. I had heard so many favorable things about her I wanted to get to know her.

"Maddie, thank you for helping Aida watch Caesarion. Iras has told me how responsible you are."

Obviously she hadn't gotten wind of the lost son/ tomb/cobra problem. I decided it was better not to trouble her with the details of that incident. It might put me in a favorable light with the Queen, but I didn't want to get Aida in trouble. Besides, I was hoping to see if she had come with any ideas to help me solve my dilemma.

"Thank you. The little guy has been growing on me."
"In just a few days we will return to Alexandria, my home and my birthplace. Have you ever been there?"

predicament. I had an idea, but I wasn't certain if she would like it, or even if it would work.

"Have you thought of any way I might impress him and make Egypt glorious again?"

"Your majesty, you are Cleopatra, Queen of the Nile. You are the richest and most powerful human in the world. Why should you approach Marc Antony with such fear and trembling?"

"What do you mean?"

"Everyone is talking about how worried you are and what is going to happen to them. It's not good to be so afraid. Show Antony the strength and the power and the glory that is Egypt. Show him the beauty and grace and brilliance of Cleopatra. Kind of like a Super Bowl® halftime show."

"What is a Super Bowl®?"

"Never mind about that. What I mean is that you should make a spectacular entrance. Something that will knock his sandals off. You said when you were younger you hid in a rug to meet Julius Caesar. This time you are older, wiser and more powerful. Make Rome want you."

She sat quietly for a few minutes contemplating my idea. A smile slowly spread across her face and her eyes began to sparkle.

"Maddie, I'm not certain your idea will work, but I'm not so certain it won't work either. We must

Rome want you."

She sat quietly for a few minutes contemplating my idea. A smile slowly spread across her face and her eyes began to sparkle.

"Maddie, I'm not certain your idea will work, but I'm not so certain it won't work either. We must begin making plans."

Suddenly she clapped her hands and the room started humming with activity. I could tell I was about to be ushered out.

"But Pharaoh, have you come up with anything to help me get back home?"
"I'm sorry, Maddie. I have been so occupied with my problems that I have not had much time to think about yours. When we get to Alexandria I give you my word we will discuss it further."

Great. I helped solve her big problem and now she was stiffing me.

"There is one thing that could help you for the time being."
"Hit me."
"I have a wonderful library in Alexandria. It contains all the wisdom and writings of the ages. I will give you complete access to all the scrolls and papyrus

that lie within its walls."

"Thank you."

As I was leaving I couldn't help wondering to myself, what I really needed was a time machine and I was getting a library card. Great.

Well old Cleopatra was right about one thing. I really liked Alexandria. It was absolutely the coolest city I have ever visited. Before we even got there I saw a tall building from a distance that looked almost like the Statue of Liberty. I found out later it was the Lighthouse of Alexandria, one of the Seven Wonders of the World. The lighthouse towered over 400 feet above the harbor. A fire at the very top burned brightly to guide sailors many miles offshore.

The city itself was built around this harbor. It was designed by Alexander the Great and was the greatest port in the world. All of the wheat of Egypt passed through this harbor. There were many canals, monuments and temples. One temple even had a golden roof. The royal city gleamed with granite, limestone and marble. They even had the tomb of Alexander where you could actually see his gold covered mummified body over 300 years old.

When we got settled in the royal quarters (very nice), Cleopatra kept her word. I was given a couple of days off from watching Junior and a scholar from the library was assigned to assist me.

The library was the centerpiece of Alexandria. It contained over 70,000 scrolls and held all the writings known to man. It was filled with scholars, learned men and students from all over the world. As far as I could tell I was the only chick in the place.

Since I couldn't actually read any of the foreign languages the books were written in, I was going to need lots of help. At first Kai, the scholar Cleopatra gave me, didn't really seem to understand my problem.

"Kai, I'm talking about time travel."
"There is no such thing. There is only now and the afterlife."

As far as I knew I hadn't died in my sleep. At least I hoped I had not.

"Look, do I seem like I am dead?"
"It does not matter what you seem like."
"I don't understand."
"According to the Book of the Dead you must struggle in the afterlife to reach your true destination. Perhaps this is your struggle. It seems real to you because it is."
"Then what are you doing here?"

Kai shrugged his shoulders and rubbed his bald

head slowly.

"I am here because you are looking for answers."
"So what you're saying is that in all these thousands
  of books, all the collected wisdom of mankind, there
  is no mention of time travel?"
"That is not true, Maddie. All books are time travel.
  They take us to places we can only go in our minds."

I couldn't argue with him there. But if I was dead or
only dreaming, why did I want to get home so badly?

Chapter 11
Sounds Like a Plan

I finally reached the happy conclusion that I wasn't dead, but I did find out a lot about Egyptian beliefs about being dead. The reason they tried so hard to preserve a body was that Egyptians wanted to live forever. They believed that if they embalmed the body, removed the guts and wrapped it in layers of tight bandages it would survive in the afterlife. That is where mummies come from. Yuck.

The mummies were laid in a coffin and buried in a tomb with many of their personal items. The tomb was packed with jewelry, makeup, clothes, games and even food – all things that would be needed in the afterlife. Sometimes even their pets were mummified and buried with them.

Finally, they were buried with the Book of the Dead. This book contained a collection of written spells to help the person fight monsters and evil in the underworld while on the way to heaven. The more important a person, the fancier their tomb, and the more junk they stuffed in it. I wondered if King Tut ever actually wore the scarab bracelet on my wrist.

I found this all very interesting, but it wasn't really

helping me solve my problem. I thanked Kai for his help and left the library for good. I decided to stop trying so hard to find my way home and enjoy my life as an Egyptian.

The time I spent in Alexandria was wonderful. Even though I spent a lot of it watching Little Caesar with Aida, we had some free time to wander the streets of Alexandria. The Egyptians were happy people who enjoyed eating, drinking and entertainment. They liked to hunt and fish and play board games called Snake and Senet. They had feasts and festivals, played harps, drums and cymbals and sang and danced. I even learned to swim the backstroke. It was easy to see why Cleopatra loved her people so much. Now I knew why she would do anything to save them from the Romans.

Finally the day came when the Pharaoh would sail for Tarsus. To my surprise and great delight she invited Aida and me to come along. She was not going to leave Ceasarion in Alexandria when there was so much that was unsettled. The only thing we had to do was keep Junior from falling off the boat. Sounded easy enough.

We boarded the boat. It was incredible. It was not at all like the long, flat boats that ferried us up and down the Nile. This was a sea going vessel, a ship that was much deeper and wider. It was going to take us three days to sail to Tarsus to meet Marc Antony.

The ship itself was painted gold and had silver oars. The sails were dyed purple and in the middle of the ship was a golden couch with a woven, golden canopy. The boat was crawling with musicians, cooks, entertainers and servants. This was going to be some show.

We finally got underway and on the second day I was summoned once again to meet with Cleopatra. I had not spoken with her the entire time we were in Alexandria.

"Well Maddie, Goddess of the Hippopotamus, what do you think of my royal sailing ship?"

"It is truly magnificent. I am certain Marc Antony will be pleased."

"I hope so. We took your idea and tried to make it better."

"What is going to happen when we reach Tarsus?"

"On the first night I am going to invite Antony and his friends to dine on the ship. The ship's dining hall will be set with golden plates, small torches will hang from the ceiling to illuminate the room, the finest Egyptian tapestries of gold and silver will drape the walls and the greatest cooks of Egypt will prepare a sumptuous feast. We will then entertain the Romans with all that Egypt has to offer. At the end of the evening Antony and each of his guests will receive the golden plate from which they ate as a gift from the people they wish to conquer."

"That sounds wonderful. Do you think it will work?"

"We will repeat this entertainment every night until Antony bends to the will of Egypt."

"Then what will happen?"

"Then Rome and Egypt will rule the world as equals. One day Caesarion will lead the greatest empire that man has ever known."

It was an ambitious plan, and I was impressed. I couldn't wait to see if it was going to work.

"And what of you, Maddie? Have you found the powerful magic you need to find your way home?"

"Not yet, Pharaoh. But I have not given up."

"My library was of no help?"

"Well, I did learn a lot about mummies, tombs and the Book of the Dead. No one could tell me anything about getting home, though."

"Perhaps, my dear child, you are home and you just don't know it."

I nodded my head and swallowed hard. The thought of never seeing my friends and family again made my eyes fill with tears. No way was I going to cry in front of the Queen of Egypt, so I just didn't say anything.

"If that is the case, you will always have a place in my court."

"Thank you, Cleopatra. Thank you for all the kindness you have shown me."

I bowed deeply and slowly left her room. The things she told me caused me to ponder my future yet again. Though I had stopped constantly wondering what was going to happen to me and worrying about how I was going to get home, what she said gave me pause for thought. It had never occurred to me that I might not ever get home again. I guess my dad would just have to find someone else to pester.

When I went to bed that night I was full of mixed emotions. On the one hand I was very excited about our arrival in Tarsus. I couldn't wait to find out how Marc Antony would respond to Cleopatra's grand scheme. On the other hand, the thought of spending the rest of my life in Egypt was disturbing.

I did have a nice surprise when I dressed for bed though. Iras had repaired my torn and dirty Winnie-the-Pooh pajamas. They were clean and folded neatly on my bed and they looked as good as new. When I dressed it felt so good to be back in my old jammies. That cheered me up a little bit. I reminded myself to thank her tomorrow.

I had gotten into the habit of rubbing my scarab bracelet whenever I felt stressed out. It was just a nervous habit and I guessed I was hoping King Tut might bring me a little luck. But this time when I was rubbing the scarab something interesting and unusual happened.

When I looked at the scarab its golden wings had parted. There must have been a latch or a button I triggered when I rubbed it that I never noticed before. I looked more closely. Beneath the outspread golden wings was a tiny compartment. Nestled in the compartment, almost completely filling it was a bead the size of a medium pearl.

I carefully removed the bead. It was so unusual. It wasn't soft and it wasn't hard either. I squished it gently between my fingers. The globule was clear and in it contained a dark, red, glowing liquid. The liquid was flecked with tiny pieces of gold. I cautiously replaced the bead, closed the wings over it and fell asleep.

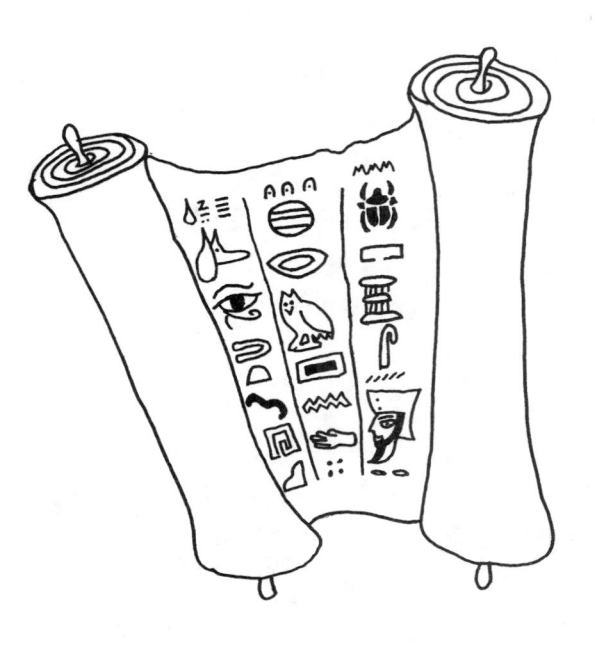

Chapter 12
There and Back Again

I slept deeply that night and hardly dreamt at all, but a few moments before I woke up I had this crazy dream about being in King Tut's court. There was music playing. I stretched and started slowly waking up. Wait. There was still music playing. It was the sound of flutes and harps and drums. I sat up in bed and looked around. Everyone was gone. We were sailing into the Port of Tarsus and I had overslept. I was missing everything!

I jumped out of bed and without even dressing I ran straight up the stairs to the deck of the ship. Of all the amazing things I had experienced in Egypt, this was the most glorious. We were coming into port and the people of Tarsus were lined up along the banks and the surrounding streets. They were dancing and cheering and clapping like crazy. Every single solitary person in Tarsus had to be there. It was unbelievable. I wondered if Marc Antony was in the crowd.

Then I looked around and realized what everyone was so excited about. The oarsmen were rowing the silver oars in time to the music. They were dressed in Egypt's finest. All the musicians were in the front of the ship playing a wonderful tune. The smell of incense was heavy in the air and the purple sails were billowed out by the early morning wind. The golden ship decked out in all of Egypt's finery must have seemed like a floating palace to the people on Tarsus.

In the center of this stunning display sat Cleopatra. She looked more beautiful than I had ever seen her. She was dressed entirely in white and she must have had half of the gold of Egypt on as jewelry. She looked like a goddess reclining on her couch under the golden canopy. Handsome servants dressed as cupids fanned her with feathery plumes.

I looked around the deck and saw Aida, Iras and Caesarion waving to the people of Tarsus. Even Junior finally had some clothes on. I caught Cleopatra's eye and waved at her. She didn't wave back, but I think she winked at me. Everything was going so perfectly.

As we got closer to the dock the cheering grew louder. Everyone was going completely nuts. I just knew any second now Marc Antony was going to come striding through the crowd to greet Cleopatra. The music grew louder, the crowd roared and the sense of anticipation was almost too much. I started yelling like a fool and waving at complete strangers. I took a step backward just to take it all in. I guess if I had to stay in Egypt the rest of my life this wasn't going to be so bad.

It was at that very moment that my feet got tangled in some of the rigging from the sails and I felt myself falling backwards. I tried to grab the rail and regain my balance but my hand slipped on some gold paint. Some idiot must have just painted it that morning. Great. As I fell backward over the railing I screamed, but I knew no one could hear me because of all the music and cheering. To make matters worse I smacked my head pretty good on one of those darn silver oars on the way down.

I hit the water headfirst and quickly sank to the bottom. The water was only about fifteen feet deep or so but it was really murky and I was groggy from that knock on the head. When I finally figured out which direction was up toward the surface I gave a good leg kick in that direction. Uh-oh. My feet were tangled tightly in some rope or seaweed or something on the bottom. I was quickly running out of air so I fought as hard as I could, but I just couldn't break free. I was more than desperate. The last thing I remember I popped open the clasp on my scarab bracelet, put the soft bead in my mouth, swallowed hard and drifted off into unconsciousness. Everything went dark.

When I woke up I was still struggling to break free and I was drenched in sweat. Someone was shaking my shoulder and saying, "Wake up. Wake up. You're having a bad dream."

"Maddie wake up. You're having a bad dream."
"What? Who is it? Aida is that you?"

"No you little fruit bat. It's your dad. Wake up. You're having a nightmare."

I grabbed my dad and hugged him as tight as I ever had. I started sobbing and blubbering like a four year old.

"Daddy, I'm so glad I'm home. You wouldn't believe what happened to me."
"Shhhh. Just close your eyes and go back to sleep. You can tell me all about it in the morning."

I must have fallen asleep in his arms, because when I woke up the sun was streaming through the window of my room. No doubt about it, I was back in McIntosh. I jumped out of bed and did a little dance and pumped my fist in the air.

"Yes!"

I went running in to dad's bedroom and jumped right on his bed.

"Uumph."
"Dad, you are never ever EVER going to believe what happened to me. I traveled back in time over two thousand years to Egypt and I met Cleopatra and Julius Caesar's son and I almost got eaten by a crocodile and I found a bracelet in King Tut's tomb and I helped save the Egyptian Empire and I almost

drowned and… Dad! Are you listening to me?"
"You are going to have to stop eating those dried
   apricots before bedtime."
"Dad, I am not kidding. I have been gone for almost
   two months and I got arrested and almost bit by a
   cobra and…"

I stopped. He was staring into space.

"What is it?"
"You're right. I don't believe it."
"You have to believe me."
"Maddie, it's Sunday, the day after your birthday.
   I'm driving you back to your mom this afternoon."

I was dumbfounded. I didn't say anything for a long,
long time. I felt for the bracelet on my wrist. Rats. It
must have fallen off in the water.

"Wait I can prove it. Take a look at this cut on my
   leg."

I pulled up my pants leg and showed him the almost
healed cut on my calf.

"Look, that's where the crocodile almost tore my
   leg off. How do you explain that, big boy?"

My dad just shook his head and wiped the sleep out
of his eyes.

"Maddie, that's why I got you a new bike. You kept wrecking your old one. Duh."

"But, Dad!"

"Maddie, do yourself a favor. Don't tell anyone else this story or something extremely bad will happen."

"What?"

"They'll put you back on your medication."

I smacked him really hard, because he knew I had never been on medication. He's the one who needs to be on something. I knew I could never convince him though, so I huffed back to my room. It was great to be home even if he didn't believe me. I danced a little jig.

In my room near the desk on the middle of the floor lay the magic marker. I picked it up and examined it. The ink was completely gone. I pushed the cap back on and placed it back in the box with the eleven other markers. On my desk was a perfectly detailed red ink drawing of the Pyramids of Giza. Amazing.

I lay back in bed and stared up at the ceiling for a few minutes. I reached over and opened my book of Egyptian history. I had to find out what happened to my friends: Aida, Caesarion and Cleopatra.

The End

Maddie's Magic Markers was written, illustrated and published by its author, David Mark Lopez. Maddie's Magic Markers is intended to be a series of twelve historical adventures. If you have any comments or questions about the books, or have suggestions for Maddie's future travels please contact the author. He can be reached by phone at 239 947 2532, by mail at 3441 Twinberry Court, Bonita Springs, FL 34134 or by e-mail at www.davidmarklopez.com. He would love to know what you think of the books. If you would like to order additional copies of either book, simply fill out the form below and mail it along with your check or money order.

Name: _____

Address: _____

Phone #: _____

E-mail address: _____

Please send me _____ copies of
Walk Like an Egyptian @$6.00 per copy
(includes tax, postage and handling)

Please send me _____ copies of
Ride Like an Indian @$6.00 per copy
(includes tax, postage and handling)

Please send me _____ copies of
Run Like a Fugitive @$6.00 per copy
(includes tax, postage and handling)

Please send me _____ copies of
Fly Like a Witch @$6.00 per copy
(includes tax, postage and handling)

Mail to:
David Mark Lopez
3441 Twinberry Court
Bonita Springs, FL 34134